Samuel French Acting Edition

Downstairs

by Theresa Rebeck

SAMUELFRENCH.COM   SAMUELFRENCH.CO.UK

MUSIC USE NOTE

Licensees are solely responsible for obtaining formal written permission from copyright owners to use copyrighted music in the performance of this play and are strongly cautioned to do so. If no such permission is obtained by the licensee, then the licensee must use only original music that the licensee owns and controls. Licensees are solely responsible and liable for all music clearances and shall indemnify the copyright owners of the play(s) and their licensing agent, Samuel French, against any costs, expenses, losses and liabilities arising from the use of music by licensees. Please contact the appropriate music licensing authority in your territory for the rights to any incidental music.

IMPORTANT BILLING AND CREDIT REQUIREMENTS

If you have obtained performance rights to this title, please refer to your licensing agreement for important billing and credit requirements.

DOWNSTAIRS was originally produced by Dorset Theatre Festival (Dina Janis, Artistic Director; Molly Hennighausen, Managing Director) in Dorset, Vermont.

DOWNSTAIRS received its New York City premiere at Primary Stages (Andrew Leynse, Artistic Director; Shane D. Hudson, Executive Director; Casey Childs, Founder) in November 2018. The performance was directed by Adrienne Campbell-Holt, with set design by Narelle Sissons, costume design by Sarah Laux, lighting design by Michael Giannitti, and sound design by M.L. Dogg. The cast was as follows:

IRENE . . . . .Tyne Daly
TEDDY. . . . . Tim Daly
GERRY . . . . .John Procaccino

CHARACTERS

IRENE
TEDDY
GERRY

SETTING

The basement of a run-down suburban home

TIME

The Present

Scene One

(A basement. An unfinished wooden staircase comes down from the rest of the house. It has a little platform in the middle of it where it changes direction and reverses itself. There are no rails on half of it. It really looks kind of dangerous.)

(There is a small, wooden workman's bench with an old set of tools, a power drill, a saw. Lots of junk that hasn't been used in ages. A lousy couch with some old blankets on it. Also a corner laundry room and a small kitchen table.)

(A door at the back.)

(The sound of a toilet flushing. After a moment, **TEDDY** *comes out. He is in his underwear.)*

(He looks around, thinks about brushing his teeth. Goes back into the bathroom, comes back out with a toothbrush. He starts to brush his teeth. Much of the time he just lets the brush hang there.)

(He goes to the table. There is an old coffee machine there. He looks in it. There are grinds in there from the day before. He takes the carafe to the bathroom, fills it. Brings it back out and pours the water into the coffee machine, turns it on.)

(He goes to the workbench, where there is an old computer. He turns it on, looks at it for a moment.)

(Then he goes to the shelf on the wall, takes down a box of dry cereal. He looks around, finds a bowl, dumps what's in there out into the large garbage pail that is stashed somewhere, and pours cereal into it. He finds a spoon somewhere and starts to eat while looking at the computer. He realizes that his toothbrush is still in his mouth and takes it out.)

(He continues to eat the cereal. Stares at the computer screen, fascinated.)

*(**IRENE** comes down the stairs. She is determined at first, but by the time she reaches the bottom step is faltering. It's not that her will is faltering, it's that she's fed up.)*

IRENE. What are you doing?

TEDDY. I was looking at this computer, this computer's pretty good.

IRENE. Teddy.

TEDDY. It kind of looks like a piece of junk but it's humming, it's got good interweb.

IRENE. Well, first of all, that thing doesn't work.

TEDDY. No, I needed to scrape some stuff off the, but –

IRENE. No it doesn't, it doesn't work.

TEDDY. It's old, no question. It's not ideal, no question.

IRENE. Okay. Please don't.

TEDDY. Don't?

IRENE. Don't.

TEDDY. Don't what, I'm being very positive and accepting.

IRENE. There's nothing to accept.

TEDDY. I accept the computer. Which is wounded and limited yes but –

IRENE. It's not wounded! It's –

TEDDY. It's broken.

IRENE. Yes. It is broken.

TEDDY. But only a little.

(He sits, looks at her.)

IRENE. Okay look.

TEDDY. *(Popping up.)* You want some coffee?

IRENE. No, I had coffee.

TEDDY. I have some cereal. You want some of that?

IRENE. No, I don't – Would you put some clothes on?

TEDDY. Why?

IRENE. Because you're naked, you can't just be naked.

TEDDY. I'm not naked.

IRENE. You're my brother.

TEDDY. I know.

IRENE. Well am I supposed to just look at you naked all the time?

TEDDY. This is my apartment.

IRENE. This isn't your apartment. This is my basement.

TEDDY. Yeah, but –

IRENE. I never said –

TEDDY. It's like where I live so –

IRENE. You don't live here.

TEDDY. Well yeah.

IRENE. You can't say you live here.

TEDDY. Okay but –

IRENE. Don't ever say that.

TEDDY. All right yeah okay.

IRENE. If Gerry ever hears you say that?

TEDDY. Well except –

IRENE. No except. This is what –

TEDDY. This is where I kind of live.

IRENE. No it isn't!

TEDDY. In between, I mean. I mean, between. Come on. It's not like I've never lived here.

IRENE. The point being you don't live here.

TEDDY. I sometimes live here.

IRENE. I'm not kidding do not say that.

TEDDY. Whether or not I say it doesn't make it true or untrue. Because sometimes it is true.

IRENE. It is not true.

TEDDY. Sometimes it's true.

IRENE. Okay let's put it this way.

TEDDY. It doesn't matter how you put it.

IRENE. It does matter how you put it and I am putting it like this. Do you know when you are leaving?

TEDDY. *(Startled.)* Oh. You want me to...oh.

IRENE. *(Embarrassed now.)* It's just, this isn't a good time.

TEDDY. A good time for what.

IRENE. Just in general. It's not a good time and and and –

TEDDY. Because I have a lot of things I need to straighten out. Not a lot of things. A few things, though.

IRENE. Can you be more specific?

TEDDY. Not really.

IRENE. Because Gerry is going to want to know.

TEDDY. Did he say that? Did he ask you?

IRENE. Not yet.

TEDDY. Good good good. Not yet. That's good.

> *(He drinks his coffee. Looks at it.)*

IRENE. Teddy.

TEDDY. Just some stuff is coming together? I just have to wait a few days, while people make their final decisions, but it's moving in the right direction. Like it is so inching forward, I'll grant you that. But it's totally going in the right direction.

IRENE. Is this like a job thing?

TEDDY. It's a little more complicated...no it's a job thing, it's definitely a job thing.

IRENE. What kind of job thing?

TEDDY. Like a startup thing?

IRENE. What does that mean?

TEDDY. I don't, you know, I'm still waking up. Like I'm not even dressed yet. I'm totally happy to talk to you about this but it's a lot to, there's like a huge story to it, not a huge story, but a, it's, there's just lots of pieces to it. I've been working on it for a long time, I thought it was not gonna happen, and maybe I stayed with it too long, I believed in the project, and I wanted to make sure I did everything I could to get it off the ground, and these people I've been working with, they were good, but it's still unclear to me how committed they were, it was like that, and I was majorly disappointed in some behavior, and I had to negotiate that and just take stock. So that's what I've been dealing with and I needed a few days to get away from it, get totally away, and clear my head, which is why, because honestly, where I was going? Inside myself? Was totally a wrong direction. The shit my brain was doing? The way it was attacking me? It's not, honestly it was bad. But I'm already feeling a hundred percent clearer and, you know. Feeling like, just, and of course so what happens? I get an email, it's all back on. They figured a few things out and they want to move ahead.

IRENE. Who is this?

TEDDY. These people I've been working with. They're good, they're okay, I mean they're not crooks. They're good.

IRENE. So what's the project?

TEDDY. You know I actually don't want to talk about it. I don't want to describe it, I don't want to be specific about it because if you say it, it could get into the atmosphere and then someone else might like feel it there. I hope that doesn't sound too crazy. Like you say things, you know how people have the same idea at the same time, it's because it's floating out there. And if you SAY your idea, it lands in the universe and someone else can pick it up.

IRENE. Okay.

TEDDY. I'm not making that up. You can say that's superstitious if you want but it's also true.

IRENE. I can't tell Gerry that. If I tell him that? He's going to get upset.

TEDDY. I don't understand what the big deal is, does he need, does he need, because let's, you know, this is not the Hilton down here. I mean it's your house too, right? Isn't it even like mostly your house?

IRENE. It's our house.

TEDDY. Well that's what I mean, it's your house too. Because the money, didn't you take the money and buy the house with it?

IRENE. I'm not –

TEDDY. I just I thought that's what you did.

IRENE. I'm not talking to you about the money.

TEDDY. Why not?

IRENE. Because you can't talk about money, you just can't. Everyone gets so angry so fast.

TEDDY. I'm not angry.

IRENE. Oh brother.

TEDDY. What are you upset about?

IRENE. *(Upset.)* I'm not upset! I'm just asking a question.

TEDDY. Well I'm asking you a question too.

IRENE. That's so unfair.

TEDDY. Unfair? I'm still in my underwear and you're like attacking me!

IRENE. I'm not attacking you.

TEDDY. It was your money that bought this house. Which means it was my money too.

IRENE. It was not your money.

TEDDY. Our mother, when she died –

IRENE. Teddy I'm not talking about this.

TEDDY. There was a substantial inheritance –

IRENE. *(Overlapping.)* I mean it –

TEDDY. *(Overlapping.)* – Substantial money which you were the beneficiary –

IRENE. *(Overlapping.)* Teddy I am not doing this.

TEDDY. *(Overlapping.)* These are facts are you going to argue with me about facts?

IRENE. I am not arguing facts with you! You want to act this crazy, go act this crazy somewhere else. You are not allowed, I am not going to allow you to act this crazy in my basement.

TEDDY. It's our basement.

IRENE. It's not your basement.

TEDDY. You're not using it! It's empty space. It's empty. It's undefined. It has no purpose. If I want to claim it, even for a few days, as a a a haven, a place of rest, a moment of calm, a cave, a life raft – I have a moral right. You know, to do that.

IRENE. Okay. Here's the problem; here's the actual problem. This is Gerry's basement. I don't care, it's true, I never come down here. But it's not my basement. It's Gerry's basement.

TEDDY. It's not Gerry's basement.

IRENE. It is Gerry's basement.

TEDDY. I don't know how you can say that.

IRENE. I can say that because it's Gerry's basement!

TEDDY. He never comes down here.

IRENE. His tools are here.

TEDDY. He hasn't touched this stuff in twenty years.

IRENE. Okay.

TEDDY. Everything is covered in dust, these garden shears? They're like rusted together! HE doesn't come down here.

IRENE. That's not the point.

TEDDY. If he did come down here he'd have to deal with, there's a real problem here. I mean I could take care of some of this for him, if he wanted.

IRENE. You want to take care of, that's great.

TEDDY. Look, he doesn't have to, he doesn't want to talk about the mess he's got on his hands here, I get it. I'm sensitive to that.

IRENE. I'm not talking to you about this. Honestly, that's just, you're just –

TEDDY. I'm just –

IRENE. I swear to god, if you try this – bullshit –

TEDDY. Bullshit? Oh my god!

IRENE. *(Overlapping.)* If you try saying shit like this in front of Gerry he will punch you in the face.

TEDDY. Which would be my point, about Gerry. I mean seriously. This would be my point.

> *(Silence.* **IRENE** *considers* **TERRY**.*)*

IRENE. Okay we are going to have to talk about this in a different way. Because you clearly think that I am going to just go along with this all over again, this is something that you seem to think has been successful for you, in the past, this mode of discussion. And I do understand that you're my brother and that puts the mantle of obligation somewhere in this situation but I'm not so sure that where you want it to land is where it is landing.

TEDDY. I'm not sure what you mean.

IRENE. There is no question that we share a history and a bloodline Teddy and it is also clear that that means something but at the same time more and more the question What reasserts itself. What does it mean. What is the obligation. What is he doing here? What is he trying to get away with this time? What is he up to? What the HELL is he up to?

TEDDY. I come to you for a few days, just a visit for a few days and now it's all, you can't do what you're doing, you can't use the computer –

IRENE. The computer doesn't work!

TEDDY. *(Angry.)* IT WORKS FINE.

> *(Then.)*

Sorry. I am sorry. I'm not angry, I'm just frustrated because you come down here and judge me.

IRENE. I'm not judging you.

TEDDY. You are judging my life choices.

IRENE. If I could figure out what your life choices are I might judge them but –

TEDDY. Oh that's nice.

IRENE. I'm not playing games with you, Teddy. It's been days. Gerry is unhappy and I have to tell him something. If I don't tell him something he is going to come down here! Do you understand that? He will come down here and none of us will be happy. We will all be unhappy, if Gerry comes down here. What do you want me to tell him?

TEDDY. I don't care what you tell him.

IRENE. I care what I tell him. And I don't know what to tell him. I can't tell him...this. I can't tell him...

(She is desperate and suddenly almost panicked. She shakes her head, trying not to cry. **TEDDY** *sees her anguish and is stricken.)*

TEDDY. Yeah okay. Okay. Look, the thing is. Here's the thing.

(Then.)

I'm sick.

(Then.)

No, that's not right, I'm not sick. I mean, that's not, the thing is – the thing is I'm poisoned. I have, my blood isn't right anymore, there's this thing that happened to me. It took a long time, years. Many years. And it wasn't an accident either, it was a person, a real person who did it. I don't actually know him, but he works at my office. Not in my office, the same building, though. The same company. And fifteen years ago, about, he started to poison me. And it wasn't like, I'm not saying that he was trying to kill me, not at first. Actually maybe he was. Anyway the first time it happened, he stabbed me with a pen or a pencil, I think, right here, in my shoulder, and it left a scar. And it hurt like shit, I mean it hurts when someone stabs you with a pencil. So I went to human services, I mean, people saw what he did, he just came up to me and stabbed me so I was like Hey! I want to make a report about this. And they said okay sure but they didn't do anything about it. And then one of the guys I worked with, he said well that was a mistake. Reporting that? And I said, why? And he was like, that dude is connected. He's plugged into the whole system, all the way to the top. He's not going to like it, you complained like that. And I said, he stabbed me with a pencil! And I didn't even realize, at the time, that the pencil was poisoned. I didn't know at first, because as I said it didn't kill me. But the mark never went away. And then a couple years later I saw this other guy, in the hall, we were just passing and then when I got home? There was a cut, right here. And it started turning colors, and then stuff, like this horrible stuff started coming out of the wound, so I went to a doctor, and he said yeah, this is bad, there's poison here. You've been attacked! But when I tried to talk to people at work about it, it was like I was the one who had made this happen! They didn't want to talk about it, or hear about it even. And then it happened over and over again, I'm telling you this has been going on for years. I have wounds everywhere. My hands shake. I can't sleep. The poison is just, I'm so toxic you can't even touch me anymore, if you touched me something terrible will happen to you.

And no one could ever tell me why he was doing it! They just said ignore it, you have to ignore it. But how could you ignore it, I was bleeding everywhere. And then, you know, no one would talk to me after a while. A few people. There was one guy on the sixth floor who always went out of his way to be nice to me. But you know I just got sicker and sicker. And I didn't want to quit, I liked that job and generally I was considered a really good employee. But my heart was infected. It didn't beat right anymore. At night I could hear it beating too hard. I didn't quit! I mean, it's not like I've resigned or anything. I wish I could. I want to quit that job so bad, I can't tell you. But I can't get myself to do it. I'll go back, I promise. Maybe if I just have a place to hide for a little while though. I think hiding is a good idea.

*(***IRENE*** looks at him.)*
(He looks at her.)
(After a moment, she goes and hugs him.)
(Blackout.)

Scene Two

(**TEDDY** *at the computer, typing.*)

TEDDY. Oh no no no no no.

(*He types.*)

First of all that is a totally solipsistic argument and second you don't know what the fuck you are talking about. Because there is not by any stretch of the imagination a framework in place to be able to support anything you are talking about. The DNA might be there in the future but that is so far down the line I'm just not going to even participate in this discussion, it's unrealistic!

(*He continues to type.* **IRENE** *comes down the stairs with some stuff.*)

Okay okay okay you can make that case and it certainly would be the right move to get in front of this, everyone is just jumping on everything ten seconds too late anymore, it's like the instant something becomes clear everyone just runs toward it and then no one can do anything and besides which the whole, it's like somebody points and goes over there over there! And then everyone runs to that side of the boat. And then the boat tips over and then no one can do anything. Stupid it's all so –

IRENE. Teddy stop that.

(**TEDDY** *turns and sees* **IRENE** *on the steps.*)

TEDDY. Oh hi.

IRENE. You need to stop that, whatever it is you're doing. That computer doesn't work. You sound crazy.

TEDDY. You think I'm crazy?

IRENE. I think you're hungry. I can't imagine that you're not hungry, you've been down here how long just eating cereal.

TEDDY. I like cereal. It's got all the nutrients you need as part of a balanced diet.

IRENE. It does not. It's just a lot of lies and sugar. I brought you some food, I made it last night. Ziti and cheese and sausage. You're not a vegetarian are you?

TEDDY. No.

IRENE. Oh good. Everyone's a vegetarian these days, and I don't understand it.

TEDDY. Me neither.

IRENE. Here you go. Here.

(She serves him a giant bowl of pasta.)

TEDDY. Thank you. Wow. Thank you.

IRENE. You know you probably should not be messing with that computer. It's Gerry's. It doesn't work but he can be particular.

TEDDY. Oh my god.

IRENE. Are you okay?

TEDDY. This is delicious.

IRENE. You like it?

TEDDY. My god, it's like, it's totally delicious.

IRENE. You must be starving. You've been down here for what, three days, you don't even come up for lunch.

TEDDY. Well, you know, I have to confess it. I'm a little afraid of Gerry.

IRENE. He's not here during the day.

TEDDY. This is really delicious, Irene. I think you're right, I think the lack of food was affecting my mood. I was getting a little depressed.

IRENE. Have you been sleeping all right?

TEDDY. Well, sleeping is overrated.

IRENE. It's not actually.

TEDDY. You don't sleep. I hear you moving around. All night there's something going on up there.

IRENE. That's Gerry.

TEDDY. That's Gerry?

IRENE. Well, it's not me. I sleep.

TEDDY. What's he doing?

IRENE. How am I supposed to know, I'm asleep! I love to sleep. I'd sleep all day if I could. God I love being in bed. We should get you a decent bed down here.

TEDDY. This couch is pretty comfortable.

IRENE. Oh.

TEDDY. No, it really is, it's fine.

IRENE. Some pillows at least. A nice duvet. Lots of feathers. It's one of my favorite things, one of those big duvets they're both cool and warm, you just wrap yourself up, it's wonderful.

>   *(She fetches some things from the laundry area.)*

TEDDY. I don't know. That doesn't sound so great to me.

IRENE. No?

TEDDY. Are you kidding? Sleeping all the time and wrapping yourself up in a giant blanket? That sounds like depression. Are you sure you're not depressed?

IRENE. *(Annoyed.)* I'm not depressed.

TEDDY. You sound depressed.

IRENE. I'm very active. I cook, I go to the grocery store. I run errands. When there's a package that needs to be mailed, I wrap it up and take it to the post office. That honestly, getting a package to the post office is a lot more work than people admit.

TEDDY. Taking a package to the post office? Are you sure?

IRENE. Absolutely. It is completely overwhelming. You don't know because you're in business, you have an office – are you still working at that office?

TEDDY. Well, I mentioned the poisoning incident, of course, which put things on a different footing. I'd call this a hiatus. I'm on hiatus but I still work there, sure.

IRENE. People take care of you when you work in an office. There's a mail room, and assistants and a receptionist. I hear about this from people, or you see it on television, there's a whole world of people who are like a hive of bees all working together to take care of each other and that package. If you have something you want to send someone, a little present, you just lift it into the air and then they get it.

TEDDY. Because the bees take care of it?

IRENE. Because everyone takes care of it! You walk down the hall to the mail room, to ask them for help, you know, putting the box together, and on the way you talk to the person in the next cubicle and you look at the things on their desk and talk about maybe what was on TV last night or what their kids are doing in school. But if you're alone. Like in a house, alone. It's just you and the box and then you have to find tape and packing materials, sometimes there are some, somewhere. Packing materials, they're kind of frightening if you have to look at them closely. When it's just you and the box it truly requires some courage. And discipline! You have to find a pen, one of those very black Sharpies, and maybe a sticker to write the address on and the post office, there's a line sometimes and the people are not very nice down there. Gerry doesn't understand why anyone would waste their time going to the post office. Well, he's not wrong. It is dirty down there. And the clerks are so rude. So sending a package, it's not, it's...

TEDDY. That does sound hard.

IRENE. Most people don't do it anymore. All these devices, you just hit a button and the computer does it all. There's a reason for that.

TEDDY. Who do you mail things to?

IRENE. Well, to you! I sent you some cookies, just a few months ago.

TEDDY. Did you?

IRENE. Didn't I?

TEDDY. I don't think so. When was this?

IRENE. Not long ago. I think. I can't remember.

TEDDY. So it could have been years.

IRENE. No. No! I sent them, to that office. It was the same office, wasn't it?

TEDDY. The one with the poisoner?

IRENE. Don't talk about that.

TEDDY. Why not? It made you hug me and cook for me, it was very useful, talking about getting poisoned.

IRENE. You made it up, didn't you?

TEDDY. I did not. No. No! Do you not believe me?

IRENE. I don't know what to believe anymore.

TEDDY. Why not?

> (**IRENE** *thinks about this, a little panicked.*)

IRENE. I sent them. I know I sent them. Did you not get them?

TEDDY. Wait a minute. Chocolate chip?

IRENE. *(Wary.)* Yes?

TEDDY. *(Remembering.)* With, like there was a special ingredient? Coconut!

IRENE. Well, that's not the only special ingredient.

TEDDY. Oatmeal. Cranberries.

IRENE. *(Relieved.)* You did get it. You got it.

TEDDY. I got it, but that was like two years ago, Irene.

IRENE. No it wasn't.

TEDDY. It was. It was several years. But thank you.

IRENE. Maybe it was that long ago.

TEDDY. *(Sudden.)* Whenever it was. They were great. Thanks. What were we talking about?

IRENE. Oh. Just, you know. What I do.

TEDDY. What do you do?

> *(A beat.)*

> *(Tender.)* Irene.

IRENE. Oh. Well. Like I said I do the grocery shopping and I cook, and I, you know, I shop, and I keep the house together. And I cook for the church bake sales, there's a real nice group down there. Although some of them don't get me started. But overall it's a nice group.

TEDDY. Why don't you have a job? It sounds terrific the way you describe offices as a sort of fantastic charming beehive full of helpful happy individuals. You have such a good attitude. They could use you down there.

IRENE. Down where?

TEDDY. Pretty much anywhere, I'm thinking.

IRENE. Gerry doesn't want me to work.

TEDDY. Why not?

IRENE. He's old-fashioned. People are still like that. Gerry's just one of those guys, he doesn't want his wife running around and everything. We don't need the money!

TEDDY. I need money.

IRENE. Well, Gerry is not going to give you money.

TEDDY. You could give me money.

IRENE. Gerry is not going to let me give you money.

TEDDY. What century do you live in?

IRENE. I live in the same century you do.

TEDDY. Well good because in this century I need money and I'm, you know, your brother. I'm your little brother, and I'm in need, I'm in need here.

IRENE. What do you need it for?

TEDDY. You know what? Never mind. It's fine. I have plenty of ways to get the money. I just, this is actually an investment opportunity, truth be told. I was offering, out of loyalty, you could really get in on something, at the ground floor.

IRENE. This is an investment opportunity?

TEDDY. That's what I'm, sure.

IRENE. What kind of investment opportunity?

TEDDY. No no it's okay, I get it. You don't have the liquidity, I get it. No big deal. Although I would like to remind you, very gently, that I got screwed in all that nonsense around the will. I didn't get what I should, and you know that.

> *(He's mad.* **IRENE** *doesn't know what to say. She goes and picks up a CD player, shows it to him.)*

IRENE. Well. Oh, I also, here's a little CD player I brought down. And some CDs. If you want some music down here.

TEDDY. Could I have a little privacy? I have work to do.

IRENE. Teddy – that computer doesn't work.

> (*TEDDY turns to the wall, sudden, annoyed. There is an awkward moment.*)

It's okay. I didn't mean anything. Come on, have some dessert. It's so nice for me to have someone to cook for. I mean I cook for all those bake sales at the church and honestly it's not the same thing, I mean they're nice down there but they're a little judgmental. They don't have warmth.

TEDDY. There's no warmth at the church?

IRENE. Not as much as you would hope for.

TEDDY. I would hope for a lot.

IRENE. Oh. Oh! I made a cake!

> (*She heads up the stairs, talking as she goes.*)

(*Calling back.*) I found a recipe a couple years ago that's a really good one, just like Mom's. It was your favorite. When you were little, honest to god, you loved this.

> (*She disappears for a moment and returns with a glorious cake.*)

Teddy, look. Look. Come on, Teddy. Just look.

> (*TEDDY turns, stops. The cake is amazing.*)

TEDDY. Wow. That's... I haven't seen anything like that since we were kids.

IRENE. Ta-da. It took me hours, everything from scratch. I'm not complaining! I loved every minute of it.

> (*She sets it down. They look at it.*)

TEDDY. Mom never made a cake like that.

IRENE. She did. We would melt the chocolate and whip the butter and the sugar in that old blender, it looked like a pterodactyl.

TEDDY. A pterodactyl?

IRENE. You remember.

TEDDY. A blender that looked like a dinosaur? I can't imagine forgetting it and yet...wait a minute. It was mint green. It barely worked.

IRENE. It was slow, yes, compared to what people have now. But we made your cake in it every year.

TEDDY. Mom never did that. She never cooked at all.

IRENE. She did. Not much, but she did.

　　　　(She starts to cut the cake.)

TEDDY. She never did anything! She was too drunk to do anything.

IRENE. That's cruel.

TEDDY. It's not cruel, it's a fact.

　　　　*(**IRENE** serves him a piece of cake.)*

She was mean and crazy. People tell me I'm crazy I'm like ha, you should have met my mother.

IRENE. She wasn't crazy!

TEDDY. Irene, she used to scream at the dishes. I came home one day, she was purple, and screaming and spit, coming out of her mouth, that was the nicest thing coming out of her mouth. Screaming at the dishes in the sink.

IRENE. There is no question, she was high-strung.

TEDDY. High-strung listen to you.

IRENE. She had a lot of energy that was not being used in the right way.

TEDDY. I'll say. She threw a mug at me once. It was a pretty one, too. Bone china. I was stunned. It was such a nice cup. Do you remember the one, with the green flowers and the gold on the handle.

IRENE. Oh my god that was a beautiful cup.

TEDDY. Right? Imagine how I felt when she threw it at me.

IRENE. What did you do?

TEDDY. Who can remember. All those years I felt like every time I turned around I was ducking.

IRENE. You don't remember her the way I do.

TEDDY. Listen, nobody remembers anything the way other people do. That's part of the problem with being in the human race.

IRENE. She worked really hard, Teddy. She wasn't crazy, she was just overwhelmed. She was so alone.

TEDDY. How could she be alone if you were there and I was there? You can't be "alone" if you have two children, Irene. I'm sorry to have to point that out to you.

IRENE. You know what I'm saying. She was lonely for male companionship after Dad left. And she was so young and beautiful, oh my god when they used to get dressed up? Both of them, they looked like movie stars. The old-fashioned kind, who always had the light falling on them in just the right way. She had this gorgeous pearl necklace. Real pearls! That was a big thing back then. And Dad, he always wore a hat. Men don't do that so much anymore and I think that's a shame. He was so dashing. And he adored her.

TEDDY. Until he left.

IRENE. Well exactly. You don't remember what that was like, you were too little. But she was devastated. We both were of course. And she never understood it, why he would just...disappear like that. Well. My point is, she could have remarried. Men loved her, she could have remarried a dozen times but nobody wanted to take on someone else's kids.

TEDDY. She tell you that? That was nice of her.

IRENE. I don't blame her. She wasn't the kind of person who knew how to make do. Some days I would come home from school and just find her crying in the kitchen, it was terrible, she would be just sitting there rocking and saying, how much is one person supposed to take? How long am I supposed to live in this cage? Her hands shaking. She was very fragile.

TEDDY. A plate is fragile, especially when you throw it at the wall. Or at me.

IRENE. Well that's true she should not have done that.

(Starting to laugh.)

TEDDY. What?

IRENE. Remember that time –

(She is really laughing now. **TEDDY** *starts to laugh with her, without knowing why.)*

TEDDY. What?

IRENE. She made that meatloaf –

TEDDY. *(Remembering.)* Wait a minute.

IRENE. And then she forgot to turn the oven on –

TEDDY. Oh yeah.

IRENE. So when she took it out it was just – raw meat! And she got so angry she –

(She is laughing really hard now and so is he. They laugh and laugh.)

TEDDY. Do you remember when, that night when we –

IRENE. You were terrible!

TEDDY. I was lively!

(Then.)

Do you remember, do you remember when Dad was still around…

(He thinks, stops.)

IRENE. What?

TEDDY. Nothing. He's harder to remember.

IRENE. I remember him. You were so little, but I was older when he left. God, I adored him. Well, of course I did. You've seen pictures of him. Well, you don't need to see pictures of him, you can just look in the mirror, you look just like him.

TEDDY. Yes but how would I know that, Mom took all the pictures off the wall and smashed them with a hammer.

(They laugh.)

IRENE. She did not!

TEDDY. I think she did, I think I saw her do that once. No, it wasn't a hammer, it was a truck.

IRENE. A truck.

TEDDY. Yes, she took this truck, it was my truck, a little, it was a yellow – metal truck. Tonka.

>   (**IRENE** *laughs.*)

IRENE. Oh my god. I remember that truck.

TEDDY. Yeah I remember, Mom was looking at something and then she put it down on the coffee table and she walked away from it and the next thing I knew she had my truck in her hands and she, you know, she –

>   (*He looks around, finds a wrench on the shelf, and smashes it on the counter. They stop laughing.*)

IRENE. That doesn't mean she was crazy. You just have to have a little compassion. When you look at things with compassion, they don't seem so terrible, really.

TEDDY. Compassion does that?

>   (*Off her nod.*)

Hmm. I think a complete psychotic break will do that too.

>   (*He goes to get himself more food.*)

IRENE. I remember being happy. When they brought you back from the hospital? Oh my god. I was beside myself, the idea of having a brother. And then of course you were just so small and perfect that I was only allowed to hold you when someone was around to make sure I didn't drop you.

TEDDY. Maybe you did drop me. On my head. Maybe that's what went wrong.

IRENE. And then when you were a little bigger you were, you were –

TEDDY. I'm well aware.

IRENE. And my friends would come over and we would dress you up.

TEDDY. Yes I actually remember this part.

IRENE. Oh my god the outfits! The little shoes. The hats.

TEDDY. The dresses.

IRENE. You were like –

TEDDY. I was like a toy, Irene, you and your friends, I was this kind of doll. Or a pet, we could say I was a pet. A pet you fed hot dogs to. Which I'm not complaining about that part. Although I will say, your cooking has significantly improved.

IRENE. I miss – it's funny, because that was so long ago, it's hard to say "I miss that." You don't really miss being twelve years old do you? It was another life. There's that funny thing they say, that all your cells die every seven years.

TEDDY. That's funny?

IRENE. *(Ignoring him.)* You're a new person, every seven years. So since then, since we were kids, we've been new people how many times? Just totally different people, totally different cells. But we're the same people too. They never explain that part. Anyway you're obviously not that person anymore, it's all just memory and who knows what that is? It's nothing. It's gone. The whole world is gone. How can you pretend that you want something that doesn't exist. I mean I know people do that. Maybe I do that. I don't know. Maybe more I just think, I think about that other person I was, when I was twelve or thirteen, and I don't wish I was still that person. But I do want to go tell her things.

TEDDY. Like what?

IRENE. I don't know. Just. I remember waking up in the morning and hearing you run down the hall to my room. I would just lie there and wait for the sound of your feet. Thump thump thump thump. It was the first sound I would hear every day. Thump thump thump thump. You were so little, and you'd run to my room, at like six in the morning, and crawl into bed with me. And then you would just talk and talk and talk.

TEDDY. And that made you happy? To have some little kid wake you up at six o'clock in the morning every day?

IRENE. It did. You were so, so…

TEDDY. I'm well aware.

IRENE. I didn't know.

TEDDY. I didn't mind the hot dogs, Irene. I was a little kid. I liked them.

IRENE. When I left. I didn't know. What it would be like for you. Alone with her. I didn't know.

TEDDY. You came back and got me. Which was a relief, I must say. Because I was getting pretty tired of the whole dish thing. Which there weren't that many left, as I recall, by the time you came back.

IRENE. She was in a lot of pain.

TEDDY. Yeah, me too. So is that what you would tell yourself?

IRENE. What?

TEDDY. You said you were going to tell yourself something.

IRENE. It doesn't matter.

TEDDY. Well, let me tell you something right now, Irene. I really have something to tell you right this second. And that is: This food is fucking delicious.

IRENE. *(Pleased.)* Oh, thanks.

TEDDY. My god. You feed Gerry like this all the time?

IRENE. What do you mean?

TEDDY. Just what a deal. To have someone making you food like this all the time. You'd get fat. Is he fat?

IRENE. He's hefty.

TEDDY. Hefty. Come on.

IRENE. It's not my cooking. He doesn't like for me to cook for him.

TEDDY. Why not? Is he on a diet?

IRENE. No! No.

TEDDY. But you don't cook for him.

IRENE. He likes to eat other things.

TEDDY. What other things?

IRENE. Well, you know.

TEDDY. I don't know, that's why I'm asking.

IRENE. He likes Kentucky Fried Chicken.

(A pause at this.)

Not just that. He likes Burger King, their french fries he likes a lot. He likes those breakfast burritos they make at Sonic. The hot dogs wrapped in pretzel dough.

TEDDY. Hot dogs wrapped in pretzel dough, who doesn't like that.

IRENE. And the place with the giant breakfast Danish. He likes that, too.

TEDDY. So, so so he eats fast food.

IRENE. I tell him, there's so much salt and fat and just terrible things in all that stuff. Sugar! I looked it up online, one of those giant Danishes, they're more than a thousand calories.

TEDDY. How long has this been going on?

IRENE. I don't know, Teddy.

(Embarrassed now.)

He's busy, he just got used to eating all that stuff and you know lots of people like to eat that stuff.

TEDDY. That's why he's so fat you know.

IRENE. He's not fat! He's hefty, there's no question.

TEDDY. Okay I'm not going to argue with you about hefty, I'll give you a walk on that. But that stuff could give him a heart attack.

IRENE. Oh well he works hard.

TEDDY. Doing what?

IRENE. It's just hard, when you're, to, you know.

TEDDY. Okay that sentence had no verb.

IRENE. He's not going to do what I tell him anyway.

TEDDY. So what is he doing that you're not telling him to do?

IRENE. Eating fast food.

(She laughs, embarrassed. **TEDDY** *decides to give her a walk on that.)*

TEDDY. Maybe it'll kill him.

IRENE. Don't say that.

TEDDY. Why not, it's true. That's what the doctors all say, you eat all that shit and it kills you. It's not like I'm making it up.

IRENE. I tried to tell him. I did. He was eating all that stuff, more and more, I would find the empty bags around the house. In the garbage, I mean, stuffed to the bottom of the garbage, in the kitchen, or the bathrooms, it was like he was eating everywhere. When I wasn't looking. I didn't know what to think about it for the longest time. I thought it must be my cooking!

TEDDY. Are you kidding, you're a phenomenal cook. This stuff is mind-blowing.

IRENE. Well I do my best.

TEDDY. The problem isn't your cooking, Irene! Who eats Kentucky Fried Chicken in the bathroom?

IRENE. I did finally say to him, honey, you know, I'm finding the remains of all this fast food, all over the house. And I told him I was worried, and I said maybe there's a way that I could help, you know, and he didn't say anything. Nothing. He just sort of looked off, like he was annoyed and I said if you're embarrassed you don't have to be. We're married. You don't have to be embarrassed. I love you, I want to help you. And then he looked at me. He just turned and looked at me, and his whole face changed, it was like suddenly just full of something and and and like like something terrible showed itself, it just came out and looked at me. It was the face of something else. Something terrible. And there was nothing again. And then he said, "I'm not embarrassed." That's all he said.

TEDDY. Wow.

IRENE. It was awful.

(A beat.)

TEDDY. You know what you just described, that's like demonic possession, you know that right?

IRENE. Oh.

TEDDY. Seriously. And it explains a lot. He's got a demon in him. I never liked him.

IRENE. He doesn't like you either.

TEDDY. No, because I'm onto him. I'm not at all surprised to hear that there's some demonic possession going on with that character. I was worried when you married him.

IRENE. You were worried that he was a demon.

TEDDY. Irene, it's not like I told you this story. I didn't come to you and say hey I saw a demon come out of Gerry's face. You saw what you saw.

IRENE. *(Worried.)* He was upset.

TEDDY. Now he's going to be even more upset. You saw his secret.

IRENE. Oh Teddy.

TEDDY. No no no come on, tell me. When did this happen?

IRENE. He's been eating like this for a while.

TEDDY. No, the demon, when did you see the demon?

IRENE. It wasn't a demon!

TEDDY. What was it like – like –

> *(He tries to make the face. **IRENE** starts to laugh.)*

I'm serious.

> *(He tries again.)*

IRENE. You can't do it.

TEDDY. I can't do it because I don't have a demon inside me. But you laugh, you know, you laugh, I've actually seen one myself. I have seen them.

IRENE. Where did you see one?

TEDDY. No no no we'll talk about me later. I want to know what is going on with Gerry, aside from the demon.

IRENE. Nothing is going on with Gerry. He's depressed, he's been depressed for a while.

TEDDY. What's he got to be depressed about? He has a nice life. He has a nice house, he has you cooking for him, is something wrong at his work?

IRENE. I don't think so. He hasn't said so.

TEDDY. What's he do again?

IRENE. We don't talk a lot about his work.

TEDDY. Yeah but you know what it is.

IRENE. He's like you.

TEDDY. He's not like me.

IRENE. I mean, it's office work.

TEDDY. Are you sure?

IRENE. He doesn't like to talk about it the way that you don't like to talk about it, Teddy.

TEDDY. I talk plenty. I do nothing but talk.

IRENE. But when it comes to work you are vague. You have to admit that much.

TEDDY. I don't have to admit anything, because we're not talking about me, we're talking about Gerry.

IRENE. We are not talking about Gerry.

TEDDY. Why are you so defensive?

IRENE. I'm not defensive!

TEDDY. You're totally defensive. I asked you a simple question –

IRENE. It wasn't simple.

TEDDY. About what you and Gerry talk about –

IRENE. He likes the television. Watching the sports on television.

TEDDY. That's what you talk about? Sports on television?

IRENE. He watches other things too. Those shows where people are so horrible to each other. He laughs. You know. When they when they...

> *(There is a pause at this. After a moment, she starts to cry.)*

TEDDY. No no no –

IRENE. I have to, I'm sorry, I have to –

> *(She heads for the stairs.* **TEDDY** *goes to her, stops her.)*

TEDDY. No no no you can't just start to cry and then leave.

IRENE. I'm fine I don't know what's the matter with me.

TEDDY. I'll tell you what's the matter with you, you're married to a guy who only wants to talk to you about sports on television and he has a fucking demon inside him on top of that, it's not a good situation.

IRENE. Stop saying that.

TEDDY. I'm not the one who said it, you said it!

(**IRENE** *stops crying. But now she can't move.*)

You okay?

IRENE. *(Half to herself.)* I wasted my whole life.

TEDDY. No.

IRENE. My marriage is ridiculous. I married a man who is horrible, he's just a horrible man. And I can't even remember why I did it! I know that it must have seemed like a good idea at the time, but I don't remember thinking it was a good idea. You know what? I can't remember anything. Sometimes I go to my closet, and I look at my clothes and I try to remember why I bought them and what I was feeling about myself and my life when I bought them and nothing is there. All these clothes. I can't remember why I put them in my closet. I can't remember what I thought was pretty about any of them. I remember the store I was in and I remember trying things on and I remember paying for them, but the moment when you think I like this, I like the color, oh that looks pretty, it's all just gone. So when I look at them all, they just stare back at me. Like, none of them, not one of them is my friend. They're all just things. In my closet. They look kind of mean to me. I thought about that one day. All my clothes kind of don't like me. And I didn't feel that way when we were kids. I remember that much. I had a couple of things, a dress with flowers on it, a green coat, that I just loved. I found a picture of myself wearing that green coat when I was in college, it was stuck in a book in a box of things that I was throwing away. And I thought oh god I loved that coat. I don't have anything like that now. I don't even love my – tupperware. And then I lie about it.

(A beat.)

TEDDY. You lie about loving your tupperware?

IRENE. I lie about everything.

TEDDY. Are you lying now?

IRENE. I don't know, Teddy.

TEDDY. Okay. Okay let's come back here and sit you down on the couch while we talk about this.

IRENE. I have to, I have to –

TEDDY. Because what it is, I think, that you're going through, is, well, you married a guy who ended up with a demon in him and that's really complicated your life here.

IRENE. Teddy please stop saying that.

TEDDY. That's really interesting what you said to me about how you can't remember thinking your clothes were pretty. Because the fact is, you don't buy clothes you think are ugly, or clothes that are going to be mean to you. You don't do it. So this is what I think happened. I think you did like those clothes when you bought them and then the first time you wore whatever it was, like a sweater, or a nice dress, Gerry probably said something mean about it.

(He is getting her a piece of cake. He gives it to her.)

I don't know what exactly, because in my experience demons can be horrible, vicious, not subtle at all. Or, they can be sort of cool and cutting. He has also managed to turn your packing materials against you. Seriously Irene cardboard boxes and packing tape are generally not hostile items. So he could have said, "Where did you put the packing tape," or he could have said "WHAT THE FUCK IS THE MATTER WITH YOU? YOU FUCKING PIECE OF SHIT! WHY ARE YOU BOTHERING PACKING THINGS UP AND TAKING THEM TO THE POST OFFICE! WHAT THE FUCK IS THAT?" Did he say something like that to you?

IRENE. I don't...

TEDDY. You said, you don't remember. Probably he said something worse. Probably what he said was so horrible you had to erase it from your memory.

IRENE. He's fine.

> (*But she clearly doesn't think so.* **TEDDY** *is cutting himself a piece of cake.*)

TEDDY. Here's the thing, Irene. This is what they didn't tell us when we were kids. There are good people in the world, and there are bad people. And the bad people aren't necessarily smarter than the good people. I don't personally think they are smarter, that wouldn't make any sense. But they will do things that good people won't do. And they know that we won't do them. And so ultimately all the good people have to hide in the basement.

IRENE. I'm not hiding in the basement.

TEDDY. Not you, me.

IRENE. Are you saying my husband is a bad person?

TEDDY. Are you saying he's a good one?

IRENE. Well he's not poisoning me.

TEDDY. Isn't he?

> (**IRENE** *thinks about this for a moment. They eat in silence. She sets her cake down.*)

IRENE. I can't even enjoy this.

TEDDY. Well that's a shame, because it's completely delicious.

IRENE. He does; he says terrible things. Mean things. Not all the time.

TEDDY. Stop making excuses for him.

IRENE. I'm not making excuses.

TEDDY. You just said "not all the time," like that's a good thing. A big break for you. He says mean things but "not all the time."

IRENE. He's a good provider.

TEDDY. Knock it off, he's living off your money. My money. You know I got screwed when Mom died.

IRENE. I didn't – I don't –

(Then.)

IRENE. That wasn't me.

TEDDY. I know it wasn't you. But it's not like I don't have a right to sit in this basement. It's not like that.

IRENE. I know.

TEDDY. And if he's up there saying get him out of the basement, is he saying that?

IRENE. It doesn't matter what he's saying.

TEDDY. But he's saying it. You don't have to say yes or no, I already know. He's saying it because he has evil purpose. Look people – I know a lot of people do that – trust me, I work in a big office, where people make a lot of money, and they say horrible things all the time. It's not so much like a friendly beehive, Irene it's more like everyone runs around scared and most of them turn into rodents. I've seen it happen. With my own eyes. In fact, I'm pretty sure why that guy started poisoning me, because he wanted me to turn into a rodent. But I didn't.

IRENE. You think Gerry is trying to turn me into a rodent?

TEDDY. I don't know, Irene. It doesn't sound good. It sounds like he's coming at you with everything he's got, and he's got a pretty full quiver.

IRENE. I should go.

(She stands, puts the plate down. She's worried now.)

TEDDY. Oh don't go. Why would you go back up there? At least down here you can, you know. Have a few laughs.

(A beat.)

IRENE. He never wanted to have children. He told me that once. It was the worst thing he ever said to me. I wanted a baby so bad. For years. We couldn't have one, that's what I thought, so I went and got myself checked, but I was fine. So I said to him, you have to go to the doctor, there might be something we could do and he said he didn't care. He thought he was fine. He didn't need to be fixed.

TEDDY. Yeah the biggest jerks that's always the case isn't it. "I'm fine!" The rest of us are like uh no you're not.

IRENE. I said, we could adopt! There are children who need families, I just wanted a child. I would have taken ten. I just... I told him, I, and he, he said he would never have a baby with me. Like that. I would never have a baby with you.

> *(She stops.)*

TEDDY. As usual, what a charmer.

IRENE. It was the first time I saw the demon.

TEDDY. Wait. Whoa, you saw it before?

IRENE. I saw that face. That face came out.

TEDDY. Whoa, Irene, when was this?

IRENE. I don't know.

TEDDY. A long time ago?

IRENE. Yes.

TEDDY. So you've been living with a demon for what, thirty years or something?

IRENE. I didn't know it was a demon!

TEDDY. What'd you think it was?

IRENE. He's not a demon, he's my husband!

TEDDY. Call it what you want, you got a big problem here.

IRENE. He still expected me to have sex with him. After saying that. He still made me have sex with him.

> *(She can't talk about it anymore.* **TEDDY** *is very still.)*
>
> *(After a long moment, he stands and moves away from her into the back of the room.)*

TEDDY. You have to get out of here.

IRENE. I don't have any money. He took the money. It went into accounts, that I don't, I can't get at any of the money. That Mom left us.

TEDDY. I have money.

IRENE. You don't have any money, Teddy, that's why you're living in my basement!

TEDDY. That's not why I'm living in your basement. Okay it's sort of why I'm living in your basement but you know, I told you, I have this thing, it's going to come through. Once I figure it out, it's going to be huge.

> *(There are sounds from above. They both look up.)*

IRENE. I have to go.

> *(She heads for the stairs.)*

TEDDY. Don't go up there. Irene. You don't have to go up there. Irene.

> *(But **IRENE** is climbing up the stairs. Within a moment, she is gone.)*
>
> *(Lights fade.)*
>
> *(The next day. The plates are still there, the remnants of the meal. **TEDDY** is at the computer. He has some Post-its. He writes on them.)*

That's interesting.

> *(Writes.)*

Fascinating.

> *(Writes.)*

Wow. As they say. Wow. Wowwee.

> *(He goes to the couch, picks up his cell phone, and starts to type. Someone approaches on the steps. He doesn't look up.)*

Hey Irene, it's about time. Where'd you go? I have figured out some very interesting things, down here. Karma is ultimately going to fall where it should in the universe. That's a theory, anyway, that karma – you know the theory. Everybody gets what's coming to them.

> *(He looks over. **GERRY** is standing there. **TEDDY** stands, quickly. Stands in front of the computer.)*

Hi! Gerry. Gerry. Hi.

GERRY. Hi.

TEDDY. Hi.

GERRY. Yeah, you've been down here almost a week now. Thought I'd come say hi.

TEDDY. Great. Hi.

GERRY. Where'd you get that?

TEDDY. I had it. It's a phone.

GERRY. What kind of phone?

TEDDY. A...cell phone?

GERRY. And what's this?

(He points.)

TEDDY. That? That's, those are...Post-its.

GERRY. Where'd you get 'em?

TEDDY. Oh. Well. Generally any office supply store carries them. In a variety of colors.

GERRY. You look good.

TEDDY. Oh. Thanks. You look like yourself.

GERRY. That's funny.

TEDDY. Is it?

GERRY. It's okay. I know there's no love lost between you and me. And I respect it. I mean, I respect you.

TEDDY. You do?

GERRY. You've always been a plain speaker. It's terrific. It's a terrific quality.

TEDDY. Thank you.

GERRY. I got to ask you something, though, Teddy. I'm going to be plain with you. Out of respect.

TEDDY. Oh...kay.

GERRY. If you can afford a cell phone, why are you living in my basement?

TEDDY. Well.

GERRY. Irene says you're having financial problems? But then what's with the cell phone?

TEDDY. It's not....hmmm. Where's Irene?

GERRY. She went out to the grocery store.

TEDDY. The grocery store?

GERRY. Yeah.

> *(A beat.)*

TEDDY. So she's out buying groceries.

GERRY. Yeah.

TEDDY. That's fun. Groceries are fun. A full refrigerator is always nice.

GERRY. You got a refrigerator down here?

TEDDY. No. No! I just meant, fun for you.

GERRY. Fun for you too, since she's feeding you now, I see.

> *(He nods toward the plates.)*

TEDDY. Oh. Yeah, she brought some stuff down yesterday. It was delicious. She's a terrific cook! Ziti and salad and a cake. German chocolate with the pecans and the coconut in the icing, totally delicious. You know when you're a kid you just eat all that stuff without thinking about it but in adulthood it doesn't even occur to you and you end up eating things like food out of machines and and cold cereal perhaps because you have fallen into a place where it doesn't matter, nothing matters is part of what we all start to believe, frankly, but you know what? That is not true, as it turns out. It's not true! Life matters. After all.

GERRY. I'm not following you.

TEDDY. Oh. Well. What I mean is, food can, it's fun to revisit childhood this way. The food we had in childhood. That feeling of homesickness, you walk through the world without feeling totally in it, you know, you're just not quite *of* it the way you used to be.

And it turns out that goes away, with a bite of cake. Chocolate cake, pecan icing. Who said this, somebody made this point already. Anyway, it turns out to be true, I felt so good eating that chocolate cake my sister made for me. Did you get a piece?

GERRY. I don't eat that stuff.

TEDDY. Oh, that's right, you like – other things. I heard about that.

GERRY. Heard about what?

TEDDY. Just that you – other kinds of food. I think she did mention that.

GERRY. *(Looking around.)* This place is a dump.

TEDDY. That couch is totally comfortable. The bathroom, so fantastic that someone thought to put a bathroom down here.

GERRY. You like it down here?

TEDDY. Absolutely. The tools. The coffee machine. Everything's very nice.

> (**GERRY** *looks around. He picks up one of Teddy's shoes, then drops it on the floor.*)

GERRY. Look, I have to tell you, Teddy. Irene, she's embarrassed.

TEDDY. She's embarrassed? Why?

GERRY. She's embarrassed, she asked me to come tell you. She doesn't want you here anymore.

> *(A beat.)*

TEDDY. She, oh.

GERRY. Yeah. It's almost a week you've been here, this isn't a hotel. And she cares about you, you're her brother, there's no question she feels that. But, you're a grown man. You can't just show up like some teenager and sleep on the couch in our basement, like that's a normal thing to do.

TEDDY. Normal?

GERRY. Yeah.

TEDDY. Normal.

GERRY. You don't get what I'm saying here?

TEDDY. Do I get what's normal? Yeah. I know what's normal and what's not normal, Gerry.

GERRY. Okay. I got to ask you something, Teddy. Are you a homo?

TEDDY. What?

GERRY. 'Cause I don't know what you're doing down here, are you doing homo things?

TEDDY. "Homo things"? No, I, no.

GERRY. Whatever it is, I don't care. You need to pack up your stuff and go now.

TEDDY. Now?

GERRY. That's right.

TEDDY. You want me to go right now.

GERRY. That's what you need to do, yeah. Irene's really, she's not okay with all this.

TEDDY. Well, I can't just leave now. I need to say goodbye to her.

GERRY. No, you don't need to do that.

TEDDY. Yes I do.

GERRY. Not really, no. She's embarrassed, she went to the grocery store, and she said to me, I want him out of here, by the time I come home. I want him gone.

TEDDY. She said –

GERRY. That's what she said. So I said, I'll take care of it, honey. It's fine. Your brother loves you, that doesn't mean he gets to just move into your house. It doesn't mean that.

(A beat.)

TEDDY. That's not what she said to me.

GERRY. It's what she said to me.

TEDDY. Because yesterday we were, she made dinner for me and that's not what she said.

GERRY. Okay look I'm going to tell you the truth. The fact is, she's scared of you.

TEDDY. Scared? Of me?

GERRY. She told me some crazy story, you told her, someone poisoned you, at your work? Like you have this whole paranoid and delusional scenario, someone at your work was trying to kill you? You told her something like this?

TEDDY. I... I...

GERRY. What you said, it scared her, how crazy you sounded, she thinks that you've really gone off the deep end, finally. Like your mom, what happened to your mom? She can't go through that again. You understand.

(A beat.)

TEDDY. I don't believe you.

GERRY. You don't believe me?

TEDDY. No.

GERRY. You didn't say that thing about being poisoned.

TEDDY. I may have said that thing about being poisoned because I was being poisoned.

GERRY. Well you can't just say stuff like that and get all surprised when people think you belong in a nuthouse. Which, my basement is not a nuthouse.

TEDDY. It might be.

GERRY. Excuse me?

TEDDY. What I mean, just because something like that doesn't usually happen doesn't mean it never happens.

GERRY. I'm not arguing about this with you. You scared Irene and we can't have you losing your marbles in our basement, so you got to go now.

TEDDY. Okay, except, wait a minute. Wait a minute.

GERRY. I just told you, I am not arguing with you.

TEDDY. Yeah, except, except Irene, when I told her –

GERRY. And now you need to get your stuff together here. I'm being polite.

TEDDY. This is polite?

GERRY. It is polite, yeah.

TEDDY. It doesn't feel polite.

GERRY. Trust me, you will know when things are not polite.

TEDDY. Whoa, what?

(A long pause.)

I'm not going to just leave my sister with you. Because she told me some stuff too, and I'm not just going to leave her here.

(Another long pause.)

GERRY. She said some stuff.

TEDDY. Yes, she did.

GERRY. What "stuff"?

TEDDY. It doesn't matter what.

GERRY. No, I'm serious, what'd she say. She tell you I'm a good provider, a good husband, is that what she told you?

TEDDY. She – said – a lot of things.

GERRY. Well, great, thanks for telling me that. But just for the record, let me tell you. I'm not liking this conversation. I don't like hearing that my wife is telling her crazy brother things about me, in my own house.

TEDDY. She is a really nice person.

GERRY. I'm not interested in your opinion of my wife. Don't, I mean seriously. Do not go thinking that.

TEDDY. She is my sister.

GERRY. That's not relevant to me.

TEDDY. Wow. That is fantastic. I mean, it's not fantastic that you think that, but it's fantastic that you would say that.

GERRY. Teddy. I'm not actually talking to you.

TEDDY. This isn't talking?

GERRY. Not really, no.

TEDDY. It's not talking.

GERRY. No.

TEDDY. Yeah okay okay but I have one question.

GERRY. No there isn't any –

TEDDY. Yeah it's just one –

GERRY. I'm not answering –

TEDDY. I really have to just –

GERRY. I'm not answering questions I'm not answering questions! This is my house. Okay. I own this house. And you've been here long enough. So there's no more discussion there's just this situation. And this situation is, it is not okay for you to be here.

TEDDY. Why not?

    (A beat.)

GERRY. I already told you, I'm not answering questions.

TEDDY. No, I'm serious, why not.

> *(A beat.)*

I'm not bothering you. I'm just down here in the basement. You never come down here. Do you need something? If you need something from down here you could tell Irene. She could bring it to you. Do you need something? Gardening shears, or a wrench?

> *(A beat.)*

GERRY. You think this is funny?

TEDDY. No. No. No! I was just trying to make the point that you can have access to all your tools and such, the things that are down here. No one is denying you access.

GERRY. I don't need to come down here. I don't want to come down here.

TEDDY. Okay so then we're back to my position which is if you never come down here and you don't need to come down here, what does it matter if I'm sleeping on the couch?

GERRY. I don't want to come down here, and I don't want you down here.

TEDDY. So it's not Irene who wants me to go.

GERRY. She wants you to go.

TEDDY. Yeah except I don't think you're maybe not telling the truth about that.

GERRY. Okay, let's look at it this way. I don't care what you think, and I don't care what she thinks.

TEDDY. So she didn't say she wanted me out. You lied about that.

> *(A beat.)*

GERRY. You know what, Teddy. I can see you have a problem here, I can see that.

TEDDY. I'm not the person who barged into somebody else's living space and said hey you're not welcome. That wasn't me. Remember?

GERRY. God you're a pain in the ass.

TEDDY. I may be a pain in the ass, I'm sure I am, but you know what? You've been seen.

GERRY. What?

TEDDY. You heard me. You've been seen. That thing in you came out. And Irene saw it. Twice.

(A beat. They consider each other.)

GERRY. I said up front I don't want him here, I do not want your BROTHER in my HOUSE but she's all, he's having some kind of breakdown, I'm going, so what? Get him out of here. She's all, he's got no place to go. You're like a rescue dog to her. She used to bring home rescue dogs, weirdest looking mangy flea-bitten curs. She's got a problem, you understand? She doesn't understand the rules of life. And now you're here. You're here, in my basement, this is a situation, I have been very clear about the rules of this situation. I gave her a few days. She told me that crazy story, what you said, so I called your work, they said you hadn't been there for a year. They said they'd really like to know where you are because apparently there were some things you took, when you left that job, that don't fully belong to you. So now as it turns out you're both crazy and a criminal. I told her, I'm calling the cops if you don't get him out of there. And she says he's my little brother. Which, as I think I just mentioned, that means nothing to me. You're like nobody to me. So I said to her, we don't know anything about this guy, I can't have him in my house with criminal behavior following him. I can't be implicated. And she says he's my family, we have history, these are, I don't even know what she thinks any of it but let me tell you something, nothing is what the reality is. I don't know how many different ways to say nothing. There are so many people out there and no one cares. There's only five or six people on planet Earth anyone cares about, everyone else is like Chinese. There are billions of them and they all look alike. You get me? People are like noise now. And you're part of that. You could disappear and no one would ever lose oxygen over it. You know what happened to those rescue dogs? They disappeared. There was no rescue for them, and nobody cared. People don't care about anybody.

TEDDY. That's rather dark.

GERRY. I think I'm being pretty clear.

TEDDY. Except you're lying again.

> (**GERRY** *takes a step forward on that one.* **TEDDY** *backs up.*)

Okay. Okay. Except this is my point, I do have a point here.

GERRY. You don't have a point. Because you don't exist. And when you don't exist, anything can happen.

> (*The sounds of someone upstairs. The two men don't move.*)

IRENE. (*Offstage.*) Teddy! Teddy! I bought a coat!

> (*More sounds,* **IRENE** *coming to the basement, entering.*)

It's not exactly like that coat I had in college, but it is green! It's not the same color green, but I love it, I think it's really...

> (*She carries a shopping bag. She stops on the landing when she sees* **GERRY**.)

Gerry. What, uh, what are you doing here?

GERRY. Teddy and I were just having a talk. He has to take off.

IRENE. He does?

GERRY. Yeah. He was just telling me, he's got some things he has to go do.

IRENE. Oh.

GERRY. Yeah. So he's packing up his stuff here. He's got to take off in what'd you say, a few minutes, I think. Isn't that what you said?

> (*A beat.*)

TEDDY. No, I didn't say anything like that. I'm happy here, I like it down here. I think it's a nice room and you're not using it, my sister's here, I feel good here. I did until you showed up and started lying about everything.

GERRY. Okay.

TEDDY. And took your truly demented psychology out for a stroll. Seriously Irene, he's got some very strange ideas about humanity. He thinks people don't exist. That thing I told you, about the demon? At this moment in time I think I have to say, I rest my case.

(There is a pause at this.)

GERRY. I asked you days ago to talk to him. Days ago.

IRENE. I did, Gerry. He's just going through some things.

GERRY. You know he stole things. From that place he used to work.

TEDDY. I didn't.

GERRY. He's got office supplies, a cell phone.

IRENE. You have a cell phone?

TEDDY. Everyone has a cell phone!

GERRY. How are you paying for it, if you have no money?

TEDDY. How are you paying for this house?

GERRY. You are not asking the questions here.

TEDDY. Yes I am. I just asked one.

IRENE. Teddy.

GERRY. They have been looking for him for a year! Who knows where he's been, or what he's been doing, for a solid year.

TEDDY. That is an absolute distortion.

GERRY. You want me to call the police, I can call the police. I can do that.

IRENE. Please don't do that.

GERRY. I have a right to say who lives in my house.

TEDDY. It's not actually your house, it's her house, you bought it with her money, which was actually my money and the criminal activity as we know was what you did in that situation.

IRENE. Teddy, shut up.

> (*Silence.* GERRY *turns and looks at him.* TEDDY *takes a step back.* GERRY *turns back to* IRENE.)

GERRY. So what, are you in on it now?

IRENE. I'm not in on anything.

GERRY. He thinks he's living here? He thinks this is your house?

IRENE. I'll talk to him, okay, I promise I'll talk to him.

> (GERRY *stares at her. After a moment.*)

GERRY. What are you wearing?

IRENE. Oh. Oh, it's a new coat, I just…

GERRY. What's this?

IRENE. It's just, it's a couple of shirts I bought.

> (GERRY *pulls them out of the bag. They are plaid shirts.*)

For Teddy.

TEDDY. You bought me shirts? That is so nice.

> (GERRY *drops them on the floor and goes.*)

Wow. He is even worse than I remember.

> (IRENE *sits.* TEDDY *picks up the shirts.*)

These are nice.

> (*He starts to unbutton the shirt and put it on.*)

And let me tell you something else. That is a terrific coat. Green is a great color. It's like a tree. It's like the earth.

IRENE. Why did you say that?

TEDDY. I like green.

IRENE. You called him a demon! To his face! You sound crazy!

(A beat.)

TEDDY. I'm not crazy. I'm not crazy. Irene! I'm not crazy.

*(**IRENE** looks at him, in despair.)*

(Blackout.)

Scene Three

*(**TEDDY** alone in the basement. He is wearing the shirt Irene bought him.)*

*(He sits on the couch. Upstairs, the sound of **GERRY** yelling. **TEDDY** listens for a long moment.)*

GERRY. *(Offstage.)* I will not be spoken to that way in my own house! I want him out of here! And I am not arguing with you about it!

IRENE. *(Offstage.)* I'm not arguing Gerry I just –

GERRY. *(Offstage.)* That idiot is not allowed to mouth off to me in my own goddamn house! This is my house! That is my basement! I'm sick and tired of being nice about this! And if you don't take care of this I will and you're not going to like it! If you ask me he should be in an institution just like your crazy mother.

IRENE. *(Offstage.)* I will take care of it Gerry.

GERRY. *(Offstage.)* This is MY HOUSE!

(The sound of movement, yelling. A thump. Silence.)

(Blackout.)

Scene Four

> (**IRENE** *is there. She has a picnic basket, which she is describing to* **TEDDY**.)

IRENE. So there's a bunch of sandwiches, there's chicken salad, and turkey and swiss, beef with tomato, I remember you were partial to that.

TEDDY. Great.

IRENE. Here's a green salad. You know. Lettuce and cucumber and some shaved carrots.

TEDDY. Yes I'm familiar with the concept of the green salad.

IRENE. Of course. Anyway. Napkins. And here's a fork. You can keep the fork!

TEDDY. I can give you your fork back.

IRENE. No. I don't need the fork. You can keep the fork. Oh and there's cookies of course.

TEDDY. Of course?

IRENE. Well, you should have cookies, is what I mean.

TEDDY. I should?

IRENE. All I mean, is I made them.

> *(She hands him the basket, takes a step back.)*

TEDDY. So I guess you're kicking me out.

IRENE. I just want to help you, Teddy. I'm trying to help.

> *(A beat.)*

And, it's not good for you to stay here anymore.

TEDDY. Okay. Okay – that asshole who you married is not allowed to just decide what everyone else does!

IRENE. He's not the one –

TEDDY. Oh stop it he is too. Yesterday you were buying me a shirt and today you're handing me a picnic basket and telling me I can keep the fork, I don't know how much clearer you can get –

IRENE. *(Overlapping.)* You stayed for a whole week, and I am so glad you were here –

TEDDY. *(Overlapping.)* – Irene! Irene, listen to me. You have to listen to me, Irene.

IRENE. *(Overlapping.)* – Teddy, I am happy that you came and I think it's been terrific to to visit and catch up, I –

TEDDY. *(Overlapping.)* You cannot stay with that terrible man! He is a terrible man and you know it and you aren't stuck here at all, you are you are you are –

IRENE. – Want you, I want you to know how much I value you, and I think I think I think I I I –

   (A beat.)

I just, I really value you.

TEDDY. You value me? You value me. That's like the stupidest thing I ever heard.

IRENE. Well, I guess I'm stupid then.

TEDDY. You're not stupid! I didn't mean to say you were stupid. But you know something stupid is going on here. Not stupid. Stupid isn't the right word. Sinister is really –

IRENE. Don't start that again.

TEDDY. Okay okay I won't call him a demon, since that word seems to fry your little brain, although it is the most accurate word and I should be allowed to use it because quite frankly, quite frankly, he is not, as I mentioned, the first one I've met.

IRENE. I can't, I can't –

TEDDY. I am not leaving you in this house with him!

IRENE. Just take the food, Teddy.

TEDDY. How can you have no money.

IRENE. Oh god.

TEDDY. That's what you said, whenever that was, where did the money go? There were hundreds of thousands of dollars that you stole from me when Mom died.

IRENE. *(Overlapping.)* It wasn't – I didn't steal it!

TEDDY. I don't care what you call it –

IRENE. You were too crazy! Do you think I went asking to be in charge of all that? There was no one else to do it!

TEDDY. I don't care about that.

IRENE. You care about it, you bring it up all the time, I'm not the one bringing it up.

TEDDY. Well because you're the one who has it people who have money don't need to talk about it.

IRENE. So that's why you came. You came here because you need money, you want money.

TEDDY. I don't care if you have money, that's not what –

IRENE. You care.

TEDDY. I'm just saying it was my money too. It WAS my money and you took it. You stole it. Not me.

IRENE. *(Breathless.)* I didn't steal it.

> *(Then.)*

It was more complicated than that.

> *(Then.)*

It doesn't matter anyway. I told you. I don't have it.

TEDDY. Where did it go.

IRENE. Gerry needed it to buy the house.

TEDDY. He didn't spend it on this house; this house is a dump.

IRENE. This house isn't a dump! I keep it nice. I KEEP IT NICE.

> *(This gets **TEDDY** to back up.)*

TEDDY. Of course you keep it nice, I'm sure it's nice but I just mean other than your stellar home management this house doesn't really have much to recommend it. It didn't cost a fortune, this place.

IRENE. You don't know anything about it.

TEDDY. Oh my god.

IRENE. Houses are expensive.

TEDDY. Okay.

IRENE. Which you would know if you ever tried to buy a house.

TEDDY. How could I buy a house? I didn't have any money!

IRENE. You had a job. You had, you had a way. I didn't have that.

TEDDY. Women get jobs now! It's not unheard of!

IRENE. I can't talk to you. Everything gets confused.

TEDDY. You can't lay that on me.

IRENE. I am fighting for my life here, Teddy!

TEDDY. You're not fighting for your life. You're fighting to give up your life. That is what you are doing; you are fighting for the right to to – just quit and give up and continue living with a demon.

IRENE. Gerry will hurt you.

TEDDY. He's not going to hurt me. I'm not the one he's trying to hurt.

IRENE. You are, actually.

TEDDY. Nope.

IRENE. Well, you have to be gone. That's the bottom line.

TEDDY. Where is the money.

IRENE. I don't know where the money is. It's not there anymore.

TEDDY. I know it's not there! That is what I'm saying!!

IRENE. You have to go.

(There is a pause. An impasse.)

TEDDY. Why don't you have any friends?

IRENE. I have friends.

TEDDY. No one ever comes to the house.

IRENE. People come.

TEDDY. People don't come.

IRENE. Gerry works hard, he needs his privacy.

TEDDY. Of course he does, he has to be able to do his evil deeds in private.

IRENE. He's not, no –

TEDDY. Why are you making excuses for him!

IRENE. I'm not making excuses, I'm trying to not go insane! You say things like "evil deeds" –

TEDDY. This is not a cheerful, outgoing person, Irene. This is a guy who has a demon in him, and I find that fascinating that he keeps accusing me of stealing when he's the one who literally, from me personally! And the other stuff he is up to, on that computer?

IRENE. The computer doesn't work.

TEDDY. It does work! And he taught it some pretty nasty tricks.

IRENE. He is a normal person.

TEDDY. "Normal," there's a compliment.

IRENE. He is not meaner, or more horrible, or more anything than anyone else! People are like that! That's what they're like!

TEDDY. That is not what they're like.

IRENE. You know it is.

TEDDY. No, that's not –

IRENE. They poisoned you at your work, you said –

TEDDY. Where is your new coat?

(A beat. **IRENE** *is stopped.)*

You love that coat, where is it.

IRENE. Don't talk to me about that coat, Teddy; that is not what we are talking about.

TEDDY. Where is it.

IRENE. It doesn't matter.

TEDDY. Where –

IRENE. It's in the closet. Where it belongs.

TEDDY. With all the other clothes. That hate you.

IRENE. I don't know why I said that to you. It was a crazy thing to say.

TEDDY. Where are your dogs?

IRENE. *(Startled.)* I don't have any dogs.

TEDDY. You did, though. You had a dog for a while, you got it from the pound, I remember this.

IRENE. I never told you that.

TEDDY. Yes you did, where'd it go.

IRENE. It ran away.

TEDDY. What about the other one?

IRENE. I never had a dog.

TEDDY. Yes you did, you had at least two dogs, why are you lying?

IRENE. She ran away too.

TEDDY. Two dogs ran away.

IRENE. Yes. Yes. Yes!

TEDDY. What were their names?

IRENE. It doesn't matter.

TEDDY. It matters to me.

IRENE. Bennie. He was the first one, he was kind of a beagle, a little beagle. And Margie, she was, I don't really know what she was. She was a mutt.

TEDDY. And they both just ran away?

IRENE. *(In anguish.)* Yes.

> *(Then.)*

I can't talk about this. You have to go. You have to go. Please please please Teddy please go.

TEDDY. Irene – listen to me. Listen to me. When we were kids you were like an angel to me. You have to let me help you.

IRENE. I don't need help!

TEDDY. Irene –

IRENE. NO.

> *(Turning on him.)*

This is nothing. You say nothing. You are not real. Nothing you say is real. Gerry is right. The things you say, they're not even lies. They're just not real.

TEDDY. They are real.

IRENE. You're not real.

> *(They stare at each other.* **TEDDY** *takes a step back, heartbroken.* **IRENE** *doesn't flinch.)*
>
> *(Blackout.)*

Scene Five

(**IRENE** *alone in the basement. Night. She sits, terrified. Stands. Paces.*)

(*She sits on the couch where Teddy slept. Picks up a pillow to hold it. Under the pillow she sees something: a pad of bright yellow Post-its. She looks at it. It accordions out. It has been written on.*)

(*She stands, moves to the computer.*)

(*She stares at the computer. She clicks on one of the keys. The computer screen comes to life, glowing. She sits for a long moment in the dark, looking at the computer screen.*)

(*Blackout.*)

Scene Six

*(**IRENE** sitting in front of the computer. The music from the little boombox is playing.* *)*

(She types. She studies what she sees. She types some more.)

*(**GERRY** is behind her. He watches her type. He watches her for a long moment. Then he reaches over and turns the music off.)*

GERRY. What are you doing?

*(**IRENE** starts, jumps up.)*

IRENE. Gerry. Oh my god you scared me to death.

GERRY. What are you doing?

IRENE. I, nothing, I –

GERRY. How'd you get that thing to work?

IRENE. I just… I turned it on.

GERRY. You turned it on.

IRENE. Yeah, I – Teddy kept messing with it. And I kept telling him that it's broken, you said it was broken, I can't even remember when that was.

GERRY. It is broken.

IRENE. Well, he must've done something.

GERRY. What did he do?

IRENE. I don't know, Gerry. But Teddy's smart. I know you think he's crazy.

GERRY. I think he's crazy. Yes I do think he's crazy. I know he's crazy.

IRENE. He's smart though. You said yourself. Those people at his work told you.

GERRY. Let me look at it.

---

*A license to produce *Downstairs* does not include a performance license for any third-party or copyrighted music. Licensees should create an original composition or use music in the public domain. For further information, please see Music Use Note on page 3.

IRENE. I thought maybe, you said he stole stuff off the computers, at his work, and then when it just turned itself on –

GERRY. It turned itself on.

IRENE. Practically. Yes. It just it just –

GERRY. Get out of the way and let me look.

IRENE. I didn't really do anything, I just –

GERRY. I said get out of the way, and let me look.

> *(He moves toward the computer.* **IRENE** *gets out of the way. She takes the Post-its with her.)*

What's that?

IRENE. Nothing. His Post-its.

> *(***GERRY*** *sits down at the computer. Looks at what she's been reading. Types for a moment. Reads.)*
>
> *(Hits a button. Continues to read. Types some more. This goes on for quite a while.* **IRENE** *becomes more and more frustrated and nervous.)*

Talk to me, Gerry.

GERRY. I don't need to talk to you.

IRENE. You do need to talk to me. Because –

GERRY. Because?

IRENE. Some of the things, there –

GERRY. What things, Irene? What are you talking about?

IRENE. I'm talking about what is on that computer.

GERRY. Nothing is on this computer. This computer doesn't work.

IRENE. Gerry come on.

GERRY. Come on? Come on? What do you mean? What are you talking about?

IRENE. I'm talking about, about –

GERRY. You better be pretty careful what you say now, Irene. Because you were the one, you wanted your brother here, your brother who is disturbed, who has created damage, your brother who is a lunatic.

IRENE. He's not a lunatic.

GERRY. Did you look at this?

IRENE. Not, no, I didn't.

GERRY. Did you look at what your brother did here? Do you know what he's been doing here? In my basement? Did you see this?

IRENE. No, I, no –

GERRY. I take care of you. I am happy to take care of you. You know that.

IRENE. Yes.

GERRY. Yes what?

> (**IRENE** *looks around her, startled.*)

IRENE. Yes.

GERRY. Yes?

IRENE. I don't know, Gerry, I don't know what what –

GERRY. Then keep your mouth shut.

> (*He goes back to the computer and starts to type, and delete, and type. For a long moment.*)

This is what I said would happen. I have been telling you, I told you, he is not well. He is dangerous. I should never have let you –

IRENE. You didn't let me. He's my brother. This is my house.

GERRY. This is not your house. It's not anybody's house if people get wind of this. I told you to get him out of here. I TOLD you.

IRENE. He was sick.

GERRY. Sick is no reason to take someone in. Sick is what you're trying to keep out.

> (*He continues to work at the computer.*)

That psychopath. While you've been running around baking cookies he's been, this is, there is – Who has seen this?

IRENE. You know no one's seen it. No one comes here. You won't let anyone in the house.

GERRY. You saw him doing this. Irene. You saw him, at the computer. Yes?

IRENE. Yes, I told you.

GERRY. It's important for you to remember that. He was the one who did this.

IRENE. Did what?

GERRY. Do you understand me, Irene?

IRENE. I understand you.

GERRY. Good.

> (**IRENE** *watches him work at the computer for a moment.*)

IRENE. Gerry. What, what happened to Margie?

GERRY. What?

IRENE. What happened to Margie?

GERRY. I don't even know who Margie is.

IRENE. The DOG. She was my dog. The dog I got after Bennie – left. They both left, they both ran away. While I was gone. Both times. When I came back, they were both just gone. I left for, it wasn't even an hour one time.

GERRY. What are you talking about?

IRENE. The dogs. Both dogs. What happened to them.

> (*She goes to him and touches him on the shoulder to get his attention. Furious now, he looks at her. She takes a step back.*)

Those dogs loved me, both of them, god, Bennie wouldn't leave the room if I was in it, he was that faithful to me. And Margie was smart, even if she got out of the house she would have known how to get back, and I was only gone for an hour that day, I was not even gone that long, and when I came back you said she had run away but where would she have run that I couldn't find her.

GERRY. I don't know what to tell you, Irene. Dogs run away.

> *(He turns back to his work, starts to type. After a moment, **IRENE** picks up a wrench from the side table.)*
>
> *(She goes to **GERRY** and suddenly brings the wrench down right in front of him. He stands up, startled, and she blocks him from the computer.)*

IRENE. WHAT HAPPENED TO MY DOGS.

GERRY. Oh that's great.

IRENE. You tell me what you did.

GERRY. You're as crazy as that brother of yours.

IRENE. You murdered my dogs. I know you did. I know it. I know it.

GERRY. That's insane, Irene. Seriously.

IRENE. I found it! After Margie. I found the box of poison, it was down here in the basement. You did it. I know you did it. To both of them. And then you left it. The box you just left it on the shelf. Where I would find it, eventually. Maybe. Not like obvious, like you wanted me to find it. But like you didn't care if I eventually did.

GERRY. You found rat poison in the basement? Maybe I was killing rats.

IRENE. We don't have rats! Except for you. Just tell me. Tell me!

GERRY. Rat poison. That's not proof of anything.

IRENE. Except that I know. Of course I know.

> *(A beat.)*

Why do you think I never got another dog. I know.

> *(There is a pause at this.)*

GERRY. Okay. Yes. I poisoned them, I poisoned them both. And then I buried them. Rat poison doesn't actually work all that quickly, it takes longer than would be ideal so I had to bury them before they were actually dead. I didn't want a dog. I don't like dogs. You decided you had to have a dog, I let you do that for a while, and then that was enough. And then you decided you needed to do it again, that's not actually on me. The first one, I accept responsibility, but the second one was your choice, you put that second animal in my way. And I'm not going to tell you that I didn't enjoy killing them both. I realize people find this socially unacceptable so I don't talk about it. But it's not the first time I've killed animals.

And I'm not the only person on planet Earth who enjoys killing animals. There are more vicious ways to do it, in all honesty, and I've enjoyed that too. But that can be messy and you're not entirely stupid. So I used the rat poison.

> (*A beat.*)

You wanted to talk? Let's talk. What else do you want to know.

> (*A beat.*)

What do you want to know, Irene!

IRENE. Why did you marry me.

GERRY. I had to marry somebody. If you're not married people look at you. You had money. You're pretty.

IRENE. (*Quietly terrified.*) You think I'm pretty?

GERRY. Pretty enough. You're malleable. You're not very curious, I like that. You do what you're told. It's easy to hurt you, it doesn't take a lot of work to do it. You're polite.

IRENE. I'm polite.

GERRY. Mostly, yes.

> (**IRENE** *goes to the desk, leans on it, overwhelmed.*)

Anything else?

> (*A beat.*)

IRENE. Teddy said somebody poisoned him. I thought he was making it up. But maybe he was telling the truth, maybe it was exactly like he said. Because things do happen. People do things that seem like there's no way to explain them, and you see them on the news and you think that's just something crazy, so far away from you, some horror in a different land. But those people have to live somewhere, don't they? You see them at your office. They live in your house.

And then you see a box of poison on a shelf one day and you think no it doesn't mean that, that's not what it means. But you never ask about it, and you never, you never...

(She stops, thinking about this.)

*(**GERRY** watches her.)*

GERRY. Okay, that's fascinating. Now, put that thing down. You're not going to do anything with it.

IRENE. I'm not putting it down.

GERRY. Look. Make no mistake here. I am not happy with this situation. You wanted some answers, I gave you answers but that is as far as this is going to go. Now give me that wrench and get out of here while I fix this.

IRENE. What does it feel like to be you?

GERRY. What do you think? It feels great. It feels fantastic. It feels AWESOME. NOW GIVE ME THE WRENCH.

*(**IRENE** backs up.)*

Irene, you give me that wrench or I will take it from you and I will hit you with it, and I will take my time and I will enjoy every second of it, do you understand me?

*(**IRENE** stands there. The sound of a door buzzer.)*

(She turns and looks up.)

They'll go away.

IRENE. No they won't.

(The buzzer again.)

GERRY. They'll go away.

IRENE. They won't go away.

   (She starts to laugh.)

GERRY. Who is at the door, Irene?

   *(**IRENE** laughs some more.)*

  IRENE WHO IS AT THE FUCKING DOOR?

   (Blackout.)

Scene Seven

(**IRENE** *on the couch. She wears her green coat.*)

(**TEDDY** *is with her. He has just arrived. He is a mess.*)

IRENE. Teddy! Hi, hi!

TEDDY. Yeah, hi.

(**IRENE** *stands, pleased to see him. She starts toward him, but he shifts on his feet. He makes no move toward her.*)

IRENE. Thanks, thank you for coming.

TEDDY. Of course I came.

IRENE. No. I mean, you didn't have to.

TEDDY. I know I didn't have to.

(*There is a moment of silence.*)

IRENE. You look good.

TEDDY. Really?

IRENE. No. You look terrible.

TEDDY. Yeah, that's what I thought.

IRENE. Here. Let me. Come on.

(*She goes to him, hugs him. He just stands there. She takes a step back.*)

I missed you.

TEDDY. You did?

IRENE. Of course I did. I'm so sorry about the way things were, the last time we saw each other.

TEDDY. It's okay.

IRENE. It was a bad time for me.

TEDDY. I totally get it.

IRENE. I've been trying to get hold of you for a while.

TEDDY. My email was down.

IRENE. Oh.

TEDDY. It was just glitchy, for a while. It's fine now.

IRENE. Good.

   (Another long pause.)

 You want something to drink, or –

TEDDY. No, I'm okay.

IRENE. You want to sit down?

TEDDY. I don't think so.

IRENE. Come sit down.

TEDDY. No thank you.

   (Another pause.)

IRENE. Gerry's gone.

TEDDY. Is he?

IRENE. Yes!

   (She laughs, delighted.)

I shouldn't laugh. Sorry. I know I shouldn't laugh. But you know. The police came and took him. He's in jail.

   (She laughs some more.)

You were right, Teddy. I found your Post-its. I found them and I looked, I looked at the computer, I did what you told me to and there were terrible, horrible, on that computer? So you know what I did? I called the police! I did!

And they came out here and they took him away. They actually arrested him, they came to the house and stood in the front door and put handcuffs on him. He tried to implicate you. But I wouldn't let him. I wouldn't. And then there was this really nice police officer, who explained to me what the charges were and that Gerry was going to need a lawyer and I would probably need one too. And oh my god this lawyer. I got this lawyer? He is a very good lawyer.

   (She laughs again.)

TEDDY. That's good.

IRENE. *(Laughing.)* So I did that, and now he's in jail and he can't come back. I changed the locks anyway. But he can't come back. He's gone.

TEDDY. Okay.

IRENE. That computer works.

TEDDY. I told you it worked. It just needed a little, there was something wrong with the.

IRENE. We sent him to jail!

TEDDY. Prison.

IRENE. Because he is a demon.

TEDDY. Well. Not all demons go to prison. That is a sad fact of our times.

> *(He looks around, confused, and then heads for the stairs.)*

IRENE. Teddy. Wait! Where are you going?

TEDDY. This isn't my house.

IRENE. But it's my house. It's my house now and I get to say who stays.

> *(She laughs some more.)*

TEDDY. You're happy.

IRENE. Teddy, sit down. Please sit down.

TEDDY. I can't. I got to, I have this thing I have to…

IRENE. You just got here.

TEDDY. Yeah, but you know, there's this project that I have been working on that, okay. It was a little complicated putting it together but it's really on all cylinders finally and it would be just the wrong thing to walk away from it. It doesn't, talking about it in the specific is not going to help you understand it. You just have to trust me. It's pretty big.

IRENE. *(Surprised, unsure.)* You have to at least stay for dinner.

TEDDY. Yeah but food is not, there's a danger. Food is so toxic, it is totally toxic now. And I've had these experiences, I told you about them, where I already have a lot of poison that my system has to negotiate. There's a lot of negotiation happening already. And it's going to be fine, you don't need to worry or anything. But I just have to be you know. Cautious.

IRENE. Oh.

TEDDY. Yeah.

    (A beat.)

IRENE. Where are you, uh, are you living someplace now?

TEDDY. Obviously. You know you don't evaporate just because someone says you're not real.

IRENE. I didn't mean that.

TEDDY. I'm aware. Oh. No worries, I didn't take that seriously. And in fact I understand why you said it. Because the question, the question of what is real is, and you know what else? Gerry was not wrong about everything. There are too many people. And reality just can't, I'm talking about a kind of –

    (He struggles for the words.)

In your heart. Or, other places in your body. Where are you. What is it that makes you a person? People don't think about – this is hard to explain. But the world is so watery. Not watery. It's plain. It's plainer than we think. When you're talking to people. Not anywhere, but pretty much anywhere, there's no way to be inside I mean, that's obvious. But when cement, there's this thing that happens when you're standing on cement. Like your foot becomes part of your brain. And it's not that you need a house, I wouldn't say that. But without the space inside the house? Not that because space is the same everywhere, it's all the same space. It's just, this other thing, that's inside the space.

    (He drifts off, thinking.)

IRENE. Teddy?

TEDDY. I thought you were an angel. When we were little. I thought you were an angel.

IRENE. I'm not an angel.

TEDDY. I know. Oh god. Of course I know that. I was just remembering.

    (Then.)

I'm not real. You were right.

IRENE. I wasn't right.

TEDDY. No, no, it's true. I'm not real.

> *(A breath.)*

It's hot in here. Kind of, why are you wearing that coat, aren't you hot?

> *(A beat.)*

IRENE. I like it. I like the color. It's green. It's like a tree. Or the earth.

TEDDY. That's true.

IRENE. Okay, look. I know you totally have a lot of things to do, and this situation with the project is important, I know that. But you can work down here. This computer works.

TEDDY. All my stuff is on this other computer.

IRENE. But you could access it, from the interweb. You can get your emails here.

TEDDY. I don't know, Irene. I really.

IRENE. Just sit down. Here, right here, on the couch. You always liked this couch. I think it's a piece of junk.

TEDDY. No, it's fine.

IRENE. Okay, so just sit here for a minute, while we try to figure this out. Just one minute.

> *(**TEDDY** thinks about it. After a moment, he sits.)*

So this is, okay. Okay. You don't have to stay for dinner. But at least let me, I made that cake you like.

TEDDY. I can't eat anything.

IRENE. You don't have to eat it. You can just look at it.

TEDDY. Look at it?

IRENE. You just stay right here. I'm going to go get it. You stay here.

> *(She goes to the steps and goes up. **TEDDY** sits alone. He looks around. After a moment, he lies down.)*

*(*IRENE *re-enters with the cake.)*

IRENE. I think it's really pretty. With the chocolate and the coconut and the pecans in the icing, the way it doesn't, you don't cover the sides, you just put it on top, and in the middle, it's part of what makes it special. Remember when we were little and Mom would bring it over to the table, we would just stare at it, it was so exciting.

(She stops. TEDDY *is out.)*

Teddy? Teddy?

(She sets down the cake. Goes to him. Sits.)

Teddy.

(There is a terrible moment of silence. She starts to cry, then reaches for his hand. He coughs, sudden, sits up.)

TEDDY. What? Oh sorry, what?

IRENE. *(Relieved.)* Nothing. Nothing.

TEDDY. Okay.

(He lies back down. Looks at the cake for a moment.)

Look at that.

IRENE. It's a cake.

TEDDY. Yeah.

(He is out in seconds. She takes his hand and watches him sleep.)

IRENE. Just go to sleep. Go to sleep.

(She holds his hand, watches him. Smiles. Cries a little.)

(Blackout.)

End of Play